Short for
Estrellita

by Lillian Rose • illustrated by Cecily Lang

Harcourt

Orlando   Boston   Dallas   Chicago   San Diego

Visit *The Learning Site!*

www.harcourtschool.com

I'm in my new school for less than thirty minutes when I hear the words I dread the most. "Make sure you print your *entire* name on the top of every page," says Mr. Cobb as he strolls down the aisle looking at our papers.

Now, those may not sound like threatening words to you, but to me they are, if not scary, at least very challenging. My name—my *entire* name—is Maria Estrellita Gloria Del Rio Fernandez. Can you imagine writing that whole line of names on every paper and workbook page at school? That's not even mentioning all the forms you have to fill out for everything from library cards to hall passes! Printed forms give you about one and one-half inches of space—two inches if they're being generous—to fit your "*whole* name." Well, this is to let the world know that some people just can't be squeezed into one and one-half inches of space.

Almost everyone in my family calls me Essie, short for Estrellita, which should be enough to satisfy most people, though it doesn't seem to make Mr. Cobb happy. It isn't that I can't understand his way of thinking, because, as he says, there are lots of kids named Fernandez in this school. There are more than a few in this classroom, including my cousins Maria Esperanza and Maria Esmeralda, and you can guess what they're called for short. That's right—Essie, just like me! In fact, most of the Fernandez kids at this school are my cousins. That's why my family made the decision to move to this district. It's fun and useful having lots of cousins to play with who are your own age and live nearby. This way we don't have to spend hours on the bus or wait for someone to give us a ride if we want to do something together—and there's always a grown-up to keep an eye on us when our parents have to go somewhere.

So that's how I got into this situation, and maybe I can get out of it by writing really skinny, tiny letters, but that just won't do for the future, when, as the expression goes, I really want to "make a name for myself." You see, I've got plans, and I'm thinking ahead to how my name is going to sound, because the kind of name you have has a lot to do with the kind of reputation you build for yourself. Doing just what? you ask, and that's a fair question. Well, as my father always says, "There are endless possibilities." Mostly he says this to encourage my three brothers and me to do our homework, because, as he also says, "Education makes everything possible."

That bit of wisdom fits in just fine with my long-range plan, which is to be the first Latina President of the United States. (In fact, though, if I'm only the second, or even the third one, that will be fine, too.) Now, it's true I can't even run for President until I'm thirty-five, so I have a lot of other possibilities before I get that far. For example, I'm planning to take a few years off before my career in politics to become the first female catcher for a major-league baseball team. I've got a few other ideas, too, but I have to be realistic and realize that making all of them happen may sidetrack my plans for going to medical school *and* becoming an acting sensation in Hollywood.

Anyway, I think you can see my problems, which are:

How is my name going to sound
    when they announce the starting lineup?
    when they introduce me at the Academy Awards?
    when I take my oath of office?
How will it fit
    in a headline?
    on a scorecard?
    on a movie screen?
    in one of those narrow encyclopedia columns?

That's why I've decided to do something about my name and do it now. What I plan to do is shorten it by choosing just one first name and one last name. Maybe I'll even use a middle initial, the way President Harry S Truman did. *S* doesn't stand for anything, though it does look good sitting there without even a period. It makes for good headlines, too, because then the newspapers can use just your initials, the way everyone knows that JFK was President John Kennedy.

Still, that leaves me with one really enormous question, and that is, which names do I keep and which do I eliminate? What I've realized is that I need help making that decision. I've been too absorbed with this problem myself, so I am seeking outside advice.

5

The first person I talk to is my oldest brother, Roberto, who's a genius and doesn't even need to be reminded that he should study because he's always reading something. He doesn't actually put his book down when I tell him I've got to talk to him, but at least he lowers it so he can look at me. When I finish talking, he considers the issue for a while, gazing off into space the way he does when he's trying to concentrate.

Finally, he turns his book over, points to the author's name, and says, "Look, Essie, this writer must have had a similar problem, and his solution was to just use the initials of his first three names." I look at the book title, which is *The Hobbit*, and at the author's name, which is J. R. R. Tolkien. I make a mental note to add this book to my reading list—first, because I know that Roberto and I have the same taste in reading materials and, second, because he is inclined to let me borrow his books.

Anyway, I thank Roberto and tell him I'll consider his idea, but I'm not sure that it's the answer, and then he reminds me of another book, one of our favorites: *The Lion, the Witch, and the Wardrobe* by C. S. Lewis. True, that's only two initials. You have to wonder why these writers chose not to spell out their entire names. Were they contemplating headlines and encyclopedia entries like I am, or did they just think their names sounded better with those mysterious initials?

With initials on my mind, I stop by to talk to my father. It's raining, so he and his crew can't do any land-scaping today. Instead, he's working in his greenhouse, where he's germinating new plants for the next growing season.

"Ah, Maria Estrellita!" he says when he sees me. Now, remember I said almost everyone in my family calls me Essie—but Papa's an exception. "Come, let me show you the rose."

This is no ordinary rose he's talking about, but one that he's breeding to be different from every other rose ever grown. The reason it has to be unique is so that he can name it, and then everyone else is required to use that name.

Actually, what he shows me isn't quite a rose yet, just a tightly furled bud, but if the project is successful, that bud will produce a blossom—and not just any blossom but, as I said, one that's different from any other rose. However, that's something that won't be revealed until the rose opens, and that's a few days away.

"There it is," he proclaims, "the Maria Estrellita Gloria Del Rio Fernandez rose—to be." Yes, that's right, Papa's going to name the new rose after his one and only daughter.

My mind, though, is on my own problem. "Papa, are people really going to want to buy a rosebush with a name that incredibly long?" I ask. I don't get an answer because he's too busy fussing over the Maria Estrellita Gloria Del Rio Fernandez rose—to be.

I abandon the greenhouse and spot my twin brothers, who work for our father after school. They're in the shack, helping the workers fill gigantic plastic bags of topsoil. The twins are so into showing off their Herculean muscles that after they fill each ten-pound bag, they hurl it into a nearby pile that's already as high as the building.

Did I tell you that most of the family calls me Essie? Well, these two never call me Essie or anything like my official names. They're the ones closest in age to me, which may have something to do with why, if they ever even notice me, they address me as "Dandelion" or "The Noxious Plant Queen." Since no one wants noxious plants on their lovely, emerald-green landscaped lawns, I get the message, so I just roll my eyes.

Del Rio Nursery • Landscaping

9

I never actually ask the twins' advice on names, because I know if I do, I'll have to listen to at least two weeks of teasing while they make up names that are even more difficult. No, I'm really just wasting time because I'm nervous about discussing this with my mother. I have the feeling that she's more responsible for naming me than anyone else, and I'm worried about hurting her feelings when I tell her my plan to shorten my name.

Finally, I head home and find Mama in the little side porch where she usually works on her flower arrangements. She greets me with an enormous smile and leans her head toward me so that I can kiss her without her having to release the wreath she's forming.

We talk awhile about how school's going and what I'm going to take to Maria Esperanza's birthday party next week, but then I feel awkward and don't say anything. Finally, I notice that Mama has stopped working and is looking steadily at me.

"So what's troubling my little flower?" she asks, using one of her pet names for me. I finally manage to express what's on my mind, but I do it while staring at my hands. When I look up, I'm surprised to find that instead of being upset, she's actually beaming at me.

"Well," she says, clapping her hands, "I was wondering when you would get curious enough about your names to start asking me some questions."

"Questions?" I say in return. "Okay, I have some questions, and the first one is, Why do I have so many names?"

"Why, you have as many names as you have aunts," Mama answers, laughing. "When you were born, each one brought you a gift—and a name."

"They did?" I ask, but of course I want to know more than that. "Mama, why did they pick the names they did?"

"For that," answers Mama, "you'll have to ask each aunt," and then she writes out this list for me:

Aunt Rosa~Maria
Aunt Dolores~Estrellita
Aunt Ana~Gloria

"Now, Del Rio is Papa's first family name, and *del* means 'from the' and *rio* means 'river.' Fernandez is my first family name, and the *ez* at the end means 'son of,' so some ancestor of ours was named Fernando. Ask your aunts about your other names." With that, she waves me off on my mission.

It's lucky the family lives so close together now, because I can walk from one house to another to question my aunts. The closest one is Aunt Rosa, who's also the eldest of the four sisters, and as always, she greets me with pleasure. I don't tell her about wanting to drop some of my names; I just say that I'm interested in knowing the source of each one. That way, I figure, I won't get into any arguments about the whole sensitive subject.

Aunt Rosa nods her head at my question and walks over to a round table by the living room window that is covered with an absolute forest of photographs of all sizes. The oldest prints are black and white, and while some are formal studio pictures, many are small candid ones. There are wedding pictures, graduation pictures, and school photos; there are grandmothers and grandfathers, cousins, aunts, sisters, children, and grandchildren. I spot a photograph of my brothers and me when we were tiny and Mama had lined us up like a staircase, one behind the other.

Aunt Rosa picks up an older photograph of a gorgeous woman with dark hair pulled back in a bun and hands it to me. The woman in the picture bears a startling resemblance to Aunt Rosa.

"That's your great-grandmother Maria," Aunt Rosa says, "who, of course, was my grandmother. When our parents died, Maria raised all four of us sisters. Of course, I wanted to pass her name on, and that's why you and your cousins are all named Maria. Besides, since the name comes from a word that means 'wished for,' it's so fitting! We all wished for wonderful nieces just like the three of you."

She puts the picture back on the table, dusting it with her hand, though it looks as immaculate as everything else in her house.

I thank Aunt Rosa and head off to see Aunt Dolores. I already have the feeling that it will be hard for me to eliminate the name of the woman who raised my mother, so I put my hopes on Estrellita.

"Estrellita?" says Aunt Dolores with a hearty laugh as she pushes a plate of chocolate chip cookies under my nose. It isn't that long until supper, but I take one anyway—not wanting to hurt my aunt's feelings, of course.

Aunt Dolores walks over to the kitchen window and pulls the curtain aside. It's stopped raining, and it's just dark enough for the first star to appear, and there it is, framed in the window.

"When your father called to announce your arrival, it was just about this time of day, or maybe a little later. I looked out this very window and thought about what name I could bring you. Then I realized it was right there in front of me—*Estrellita*, the little star."

Aunt Dolores looks at me with that all-knowing expression she sometimes has and says, "I think it's a name that is full of promise, just as you are."

I still have time to get to Aunt Ana's house to find out about Gloria, which is really my last hope.

"Gloria, Gloria, that wonderful woman," Aunt Ana keeps repeating after I pose my question. I politely turn down her invitation to stay for supper and wait for her to explain Gloria to me.

Aunt Ana proceeds with her supper preparations as she speaks. "I was in the second grade, just a little girl, but with an enormous problem. I was convinced that I was the only child in the world who couldn't learn to read a book. I just couldn't seem to read the words the way I was supposed to. I felt like giving up, but the teacher—Gloria Thompson was her name—had another idea. What an appropriate name! *Gloria* can mean 'blessing,' you know. She said that I should have my eyes examined, and I did. Do you know what they found?"

Of course I don't know, but I can tell where this is going. It's while Aunt Ana is explaining how getting glasses helped her read, get good grades, and make her family proud that I finally come to a decision about how my name will appear in the record books. From now on, I promise myself firmly, I will always be Maria Estrellita Gloria Del Rio Fernandez.

After all, every one of my names has a history I can't ignore, and maybe, as Aunt Dolores says, my name also has a promising future. However, in the meantime, I'll continue to answer to Essie, which is short for Estrellita.

Maria
Estrellita
Gloria
Del Rio
Fernandez